101 DALMATIANS

Ladybird Books

Pongo the Dalmatian lived with a young man called Roger Radcliff, in a cosy flat in London. Roger was a musician and spent most of his time at the piano making up songs. He wasn't very good at it.

Pongo sometimes wished his master would find a girlfriend – then maybe he'd spend less time playing those awful songs!

First edition

Published by Ladybird Books Ltd Loughborough Leicestershire UK

Printed in England (3)

One day when Roger and Pongo were out for a walk, they met a pretty young lady called Anita. And Anita had a beautiful female Dalmatian called Perdita with her!

Roger and Anita soon fell in love and got married. Pongo was thrilled, for he and Perdita had fallen in love, too.

Everything went well until someone called Cruella De Vil came to visit. She said she was a friend of Anita's, but Roger and Anita didn't like her, and she frightened Perdita and Pongo.

As she was leaving, Cruella looked at the dogs and said, "I hear Perdita's expecting. When are the puppies due?"

"In three weeks," said Anita.

"You know, I *love* Dalmatian puppies," said Cruella. "You will let me have them all, won't you?" Then she drove off with a smug smile.

Dalmatians usually have six or seven
puppies, but Perdita had FIFTEEN!
Everyone was delighted, especially
Nanny, the maid – she was going to help
look after the puppies.

Just two months later, Cruella turned up again. "I hear Perdita has had *fifteen* puppies!" she said. "Name your price. I'll buy them all." And she took out her cheque book and pen.

"Oh no, you won't," said Roger. "We're not selling a single one."

"Rubbish!" shouted Cruella, shaking her pen angrily. The ink that spattered out turned Roger into something of a Dalmatian himself, and even gave Pongo a few extra spots!

Roger was so furious he pushed Cruella out of the house. "And don't *ever* come back!" he shouted after her.

Pongo and Perdita were overjoyed when they heard that none of their puppies would be sold. Their beloved family was safe.

Nanny was delighted, too. She was devoted to the puppies, and would have hated losing a single one. That evening, as she tucked the puppies into their big basket in the kitchen, she gave each one of them an extra cuddle. "There you are," she said gently, as she put the last puppy to bed. "Good night and sweet dreams."

But no one would have been very happy
if they had known what Cruella was
planning. It all happened very quickly.

Once the puppies were in bed, Roger
and Anita took Pongo and Perdita
for their walk.

They didn't notice the
van that was
parked close
to the house.
And they didn't
notice the two
evil-looking
men in the van,
Horace and
Jasper Badun.

As soon as Roger and Anita and the dogs disappeared round the corner, the Baduns went to the house and rang the bell. Nanny opened the door.

"Good evening madam," said the men politely. "We've come about the electricity."

"At this time of night?" snorted Nanny. "Come back tomorrow!"

But Horace
and Jasper
forced their way
in. They put a gag in
Nanny's mouth, tied her
up and shoved her into
the broom cupboard.

Poor Nanny couldn't see anything, but
she could hear the Baduns moving
about. And she could hear the
frightened barking of the puppies as
they were stuffed into a big sack.

By the time Roger and Anita got
back with Pongo and Perdita, it
was too late. The big basket in
the kitchen was
empty, and the
puppies were
gone. The Baduns'
van had long
since disappeared.

Perdita and Pongo looked at each other. It was up to them to find their missing family.

As soon as they could, they went to their neighbour Dan, a Great Dane, and his terrier friend. The two dogs were very angry when they heard what had happened.

"The villains!" growled Dan. "We won't let them get away with this."

And he and his friend went off to send out an all-dog alert about the kidnapped puppies.

The news spread across London and out into the countryside, until it reached a big old dog called Colonel and his cat friend, Sergeant Tibs.

"I heard a lot of puppies barking in the old De Vil house last night," said Colonel. "Let's go have a look."

Tibs climbed onto Colonel's back, and the two set off to investigate.

When they got to Cruella's big, gloomy mansion, Colonel and Sergeant Tibs crept up to a lighted window. Inside, they saw Jasper Badun sitting and watching television.

But he wasn't the only one watching television.

All round
the room were
Dalmatian puppies,
their eyes glued to
the screen. There
weren't just fifteen,
or forty or even fifty.
There were at least
eighty of them!

News that the puppies had been found travelled quickly back to Pongo and Perdita.

"We must go and rescue them right away," they told Dan.

"Right," said Dan, "I'll wait here for you. And I'll notify some friends, in case you need help along the way."

Meanwhile, at the De Vil house, Sergeant Tibs and Colonel saw Jasper Badun sit down to watch television with his brother. Then they saw Cruella drive up and go inside.

"You lazy good-for-nothings!" Cruella shouted at the Baduns. "You're supposed to be working! I want the skins of all these puppies for fur coats. And I want them ready by the morning!"

Fur coats from puppy skins? What a horrible thought! Colonel and Sergeant Tibs knew there was no time to lose.

Tibs crept in through an open window. "You're all in danger," he whispered to the puppies. "Follow me – *quietly*!"

But one puppy suddenly yelped with excitement, and the Baduns swung round to look. When they saw the puppies escaping, they jumped up and tried to stop them.

Just at that moment, Pongo and Perdita arrived. Bounding into action, Perdita helped one of the puppies pull the carpet from under the Baduns' feet. Horace fell into the fire, where he got very hot and bothered indeed.

While the fighting continued, Tibs led the puppies out of the house and along to the stable.

Perdita and Pongo
couldn't believe it
when they counted the
puppies. Then Colonel
explained what Cruella
had wanted to do with
them all.

"We'll take all the
puppies back home
with us," said Perdita.
"They'll be safe with
Roger and Anita."

While the puppies were being
counted all over again, the Baduns
rushed past. They knew how furious
Cruella would be, and they were
desperately trying to find the puppies.
Fortunately, Colonel managed to keep
the men out of the stable.

As soon as the Baduns
were out of sight, Pongo,
Perdita and all the puppies
set off for home.

It was bitterly cold in the fields and woods, and there was snow on the ground, which made walking difficult. The puppies soon grew cold and very tired.

When Pongo spotted a farmhouse, they decided to stop. The farm's guard dog gave them a friendly welcome.

"Bring the puppies to the hayloft," he said. "They'll soon get warm there, and then they can have a nice sleep."

Next morning the journey began again.
Pongo, at the end of the line, swept
away their tracks to confuse anyone who
might be following them.

Suddenly the dogs stopped and pricked up their ears. They could hear a car engine.

"Quick, in here! Come into my barn!" urged a friendly Labrador. As the last puppy raced into the barn, a car stopped just outside.

It was Cruella. "I'll catch those wretched dogs!" they heard her say. But the barn door was closed, and she didn't see them.

Inside the barn, the
Dalmatians wondered
how they would escape.

"Don't worry," said the
Labrador. "There's a
lorry leaving this farm
for London. It will
take you back home."

Then he looked at them all and grinned. "You know," he said, "with those spots, that nasty lady will see you a mile off. But if you were all Labradors like me, she'd never recognise you."

He led them to a big heap of soot in a corner of the barn. "Everyone roll in this!" he ordered.

The puppies thought it was a great idea. And in no time at all, the Dalmatians became Labradors!

The Dalmatians left the barn and hurried past Cruella's car, hoping their disguise would fool her.

At first it seemed to be working. But then disaster struck! It began to rain.

Cruella stared in amazement as white spots began to appear on the 'Labradors'. The rain was washing away the soot!

The Dalmatians really
had no time to lose now!
Before Cruella even had
a chance to move, the
dogs all jumped into the
lorry bound for London.
Luckily, it started off
at once.

"I'll catch you yet!"
screamed Cruella. She
started her car and, with
her tyres skidding and
screeching, went tearing
after the lorry.

The lorry sped along, while Pongo watched anxiously out of the back. Cruella was beginning to gain on them.

However, neither Pongo nor Cruella noticed the Baduns' van heading towards them. As Cruella pulled out to pass the lorry – *WHAM!*

The Baduns' van crashed
right into Cruella's car,
and they all went over
a cliff together. The
villains were never
seen again.

Later that day the lorry reached London.
Pongo and Perdita were so excited. What
a surprise they were going to give Roger
and Anita!

But Anita was more frightened than
surprised when a big 'Labrador' ran into
the house. She didn't realise it was
Perdita!

Then all the puppies came racing in, too,
with Pongo calmly bringing up the rear.

Roger recognised them right away. He was so pleased he sat down at the piano straightaway to write a song about their adventures!

Anita couldn't believe what a lot of them there were. Ninety nine puppies plus Pongo and Perdita – that made one hundred and one Dalmatians.

"Oh my goodness!" said Nanny. "It'll take me all night to put them to bed!"